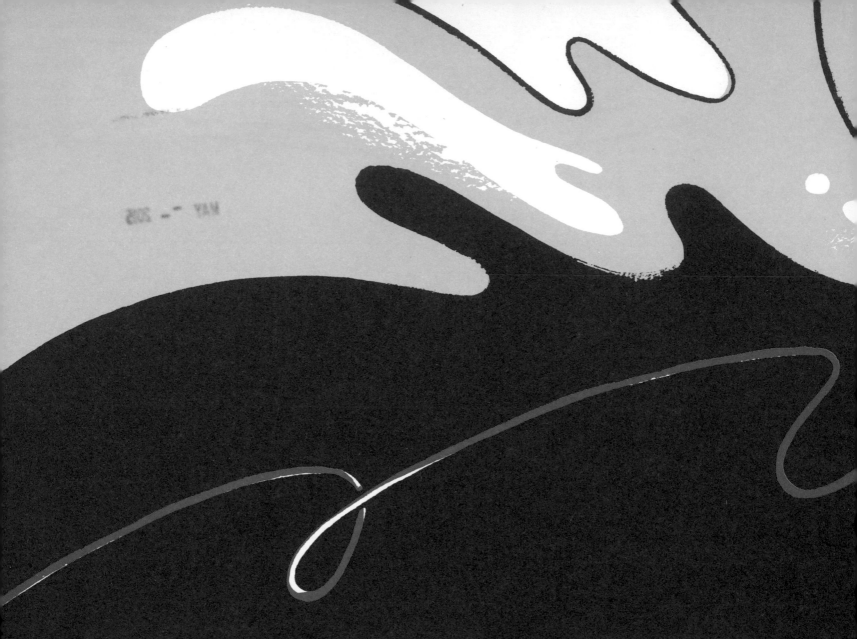

Her Idea

©2015 Flying Eye Books
Order from flyingeyebooks.com

Text and Artwork
©2010 Rilla Alexander
Visit **sozi.com** and **byrilla.com**

Published by **Flying Eye Books**
an imprint of Nobrow Ltd.
62 Great Eastern Street
London **EC2A3QR**

Printed in Poland

ISBN 978-1-909263-40-6

All rights reserved. No part of this
publication may be reproduced or
transmitted in any form or by any
means, electronic or mechanical,
including photocopying, recording
or by any information and storage
retrieval system without prior written
consent from the publisher or author.

FSC
www.fsc.org
MIX
Paper from
responsible sources
FSC® C118475

Flying Eye Books

Her idea

by Rilla

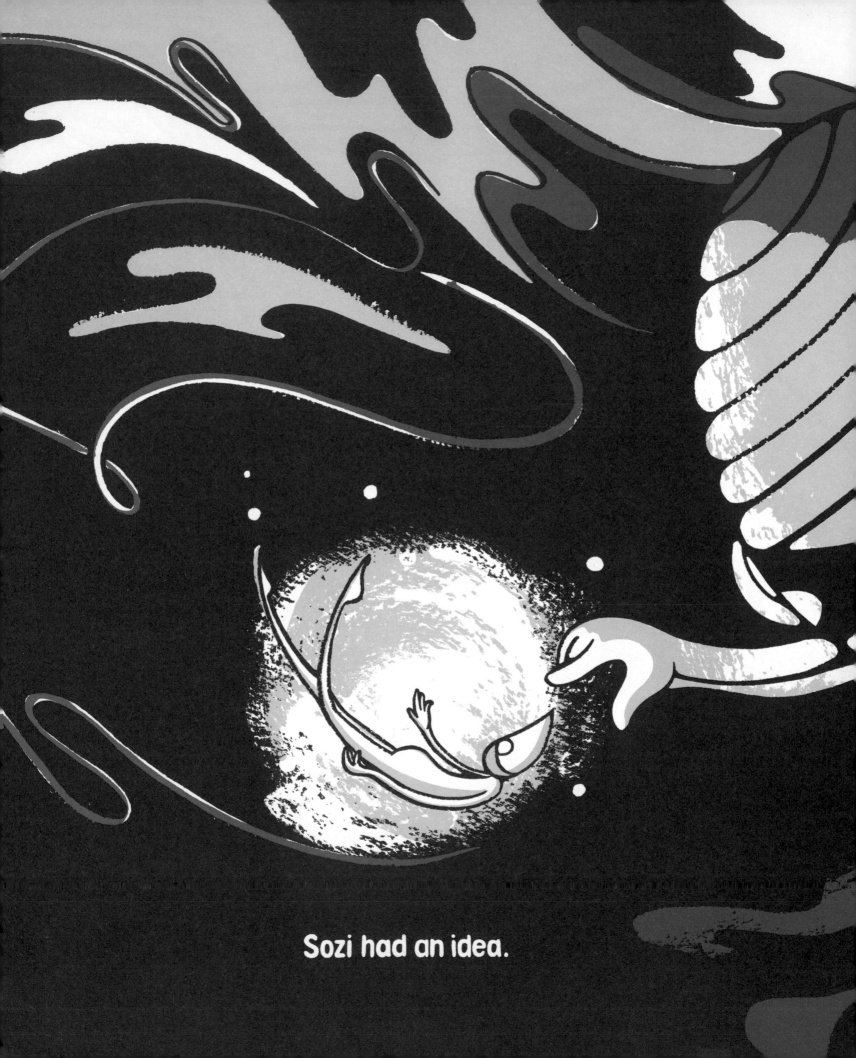

Sozi had an idea.

In fact, she had hundreds.

They came to her everywhere,
anytime her mind wandered.

Her head was swimming with them (all slippery and slimey).

Some were simple and smart,
others silly and surprising.

**The newest idea was always the best.
She loved every one of them more than the rest.**

If she only had
time, they would
be such fun...

One thing was sure,
something had to be done.

It was time to begin!

She was set to start.
She was going to make a work of art.

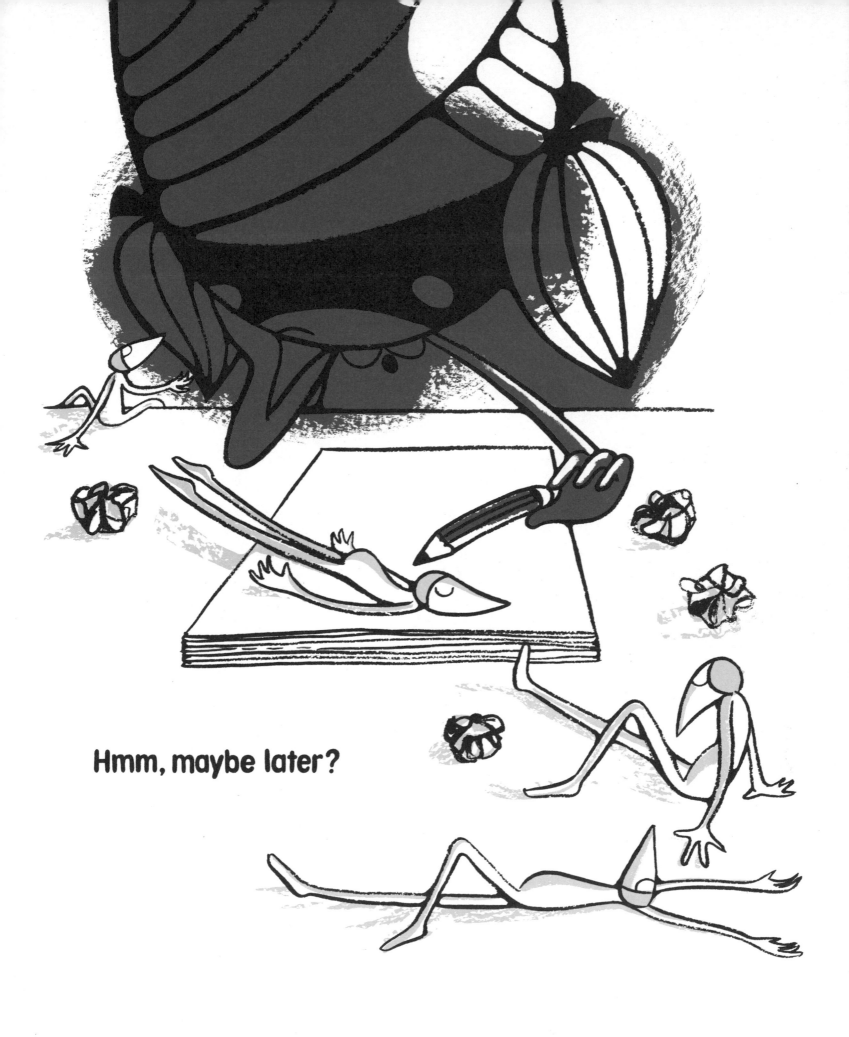

Hmm, maybe later?

Not today anyway.

It was such a big task
and she'd much rather play.

**Slowly and surely,
one by one,
the ideas slipped away...**

...until there were none.

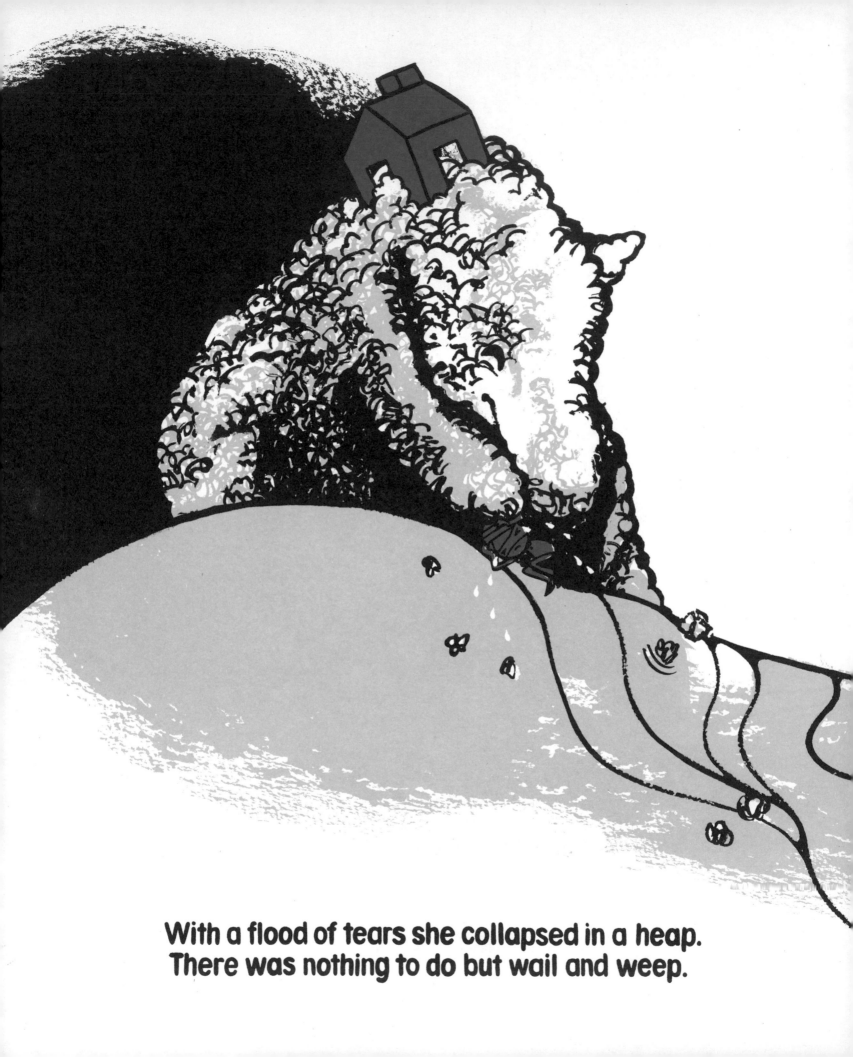

**With a flood of tears she collapsed in a heap.
There was nothing to do but wail and weep.**

She had no ideas. She couldn't cope...
until a kind passerby stopped to offer some hope.

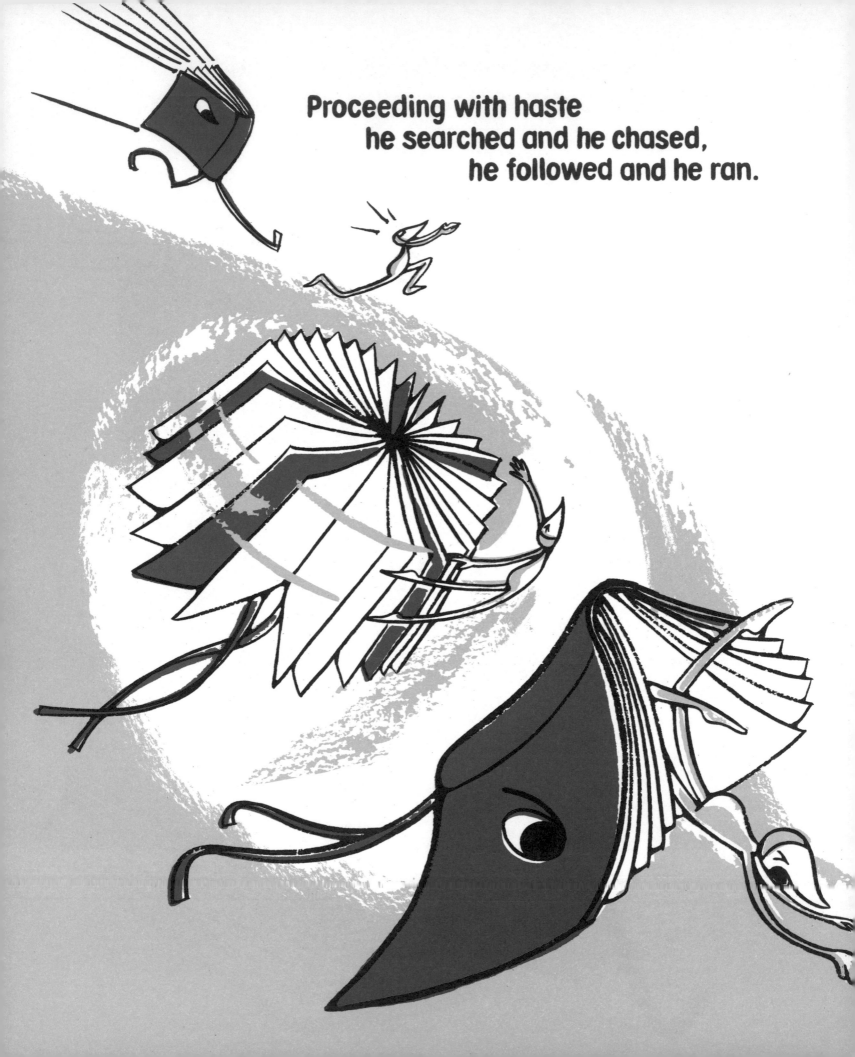

Proceeding with haste
he searched and he chased,
he followed and he ran.

And when, at last,
    he caught that idea
        there was an almighty,
            earth-shaking...

He gave Sozi the idea
squished for safekeeping,
caught in the moment
as it was leaping.

Sozi's eyes lit up.
She hugged her new friend,
"Oh please, oh please,
can we do that again?!"

...they found those ideas everywhere!

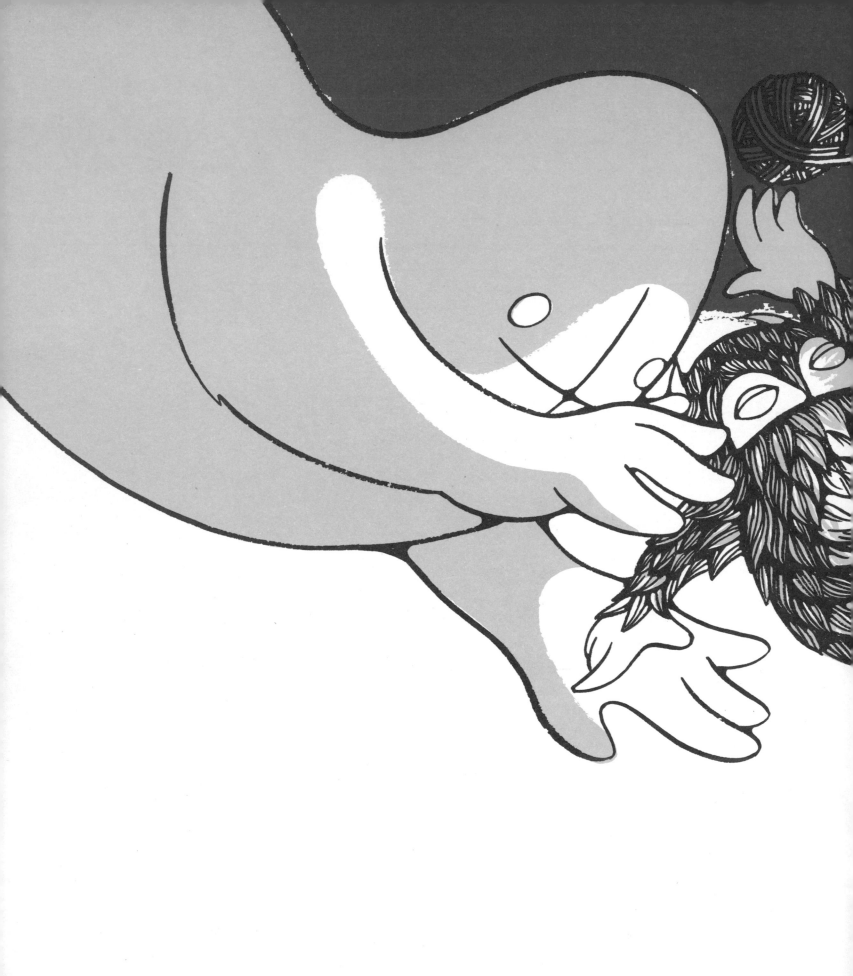

And not just ideas, but other stuff too,
that might come in handy. Who knew?

Happy at last, her mind was now clear.
She looked through the pages of captured ideas.

There was an idea for a book. That was the one!
She made a plan to get it done.

Yet even after she
finished the start

and worked till
half past the middle

she still didn't know
what'd be at THE END

and if she'd have
to begin again.

But she kept on regardless.
She refused to quit.

When THE END came,
that's when she would deal with it!

So what did she find when
she reached the last page?

Cheering crowds, a parade, an award on a stage?

No. You wouldn't guess what she found at THE END.

There was no-one there except her idea book friend.

He opened up proudly to give her a hug.
But then without warning, signal or clue...

He squished her.
Believe it... it's true!

But dear reader, don't fret and don't fear.
We all know, after all, this was her idea!

Living in a book along with her friends...
that's the way this story ends.

And here at THE END (the very last one)
this is **Her Idea** and it's completely **done!**